GILLBERT

#1 "The Little Merman"
By Art Baltazar
Production – Manosaur Martin
Assistant Managing Editor – Jeff Whitman
Jim Salicrup
Editor-in-Chief

SHERBERT   ALBERT

Papercutz books may be purchased for business or promotional use. For information on bulk purchases please contact Macmillan Corporate and Premium Sales Department at (800) 221-795 x5442.

Hardcover ISBN: 978-1-5458-0144-4
Paperback ISBN: 978-1-5458-0145-1

Printed in India
September 2018

Distributed by Macmillan
First Printing

KING NAUTICUS

CURLY   SHARK   SEA
BOO   BUG   BUNNY

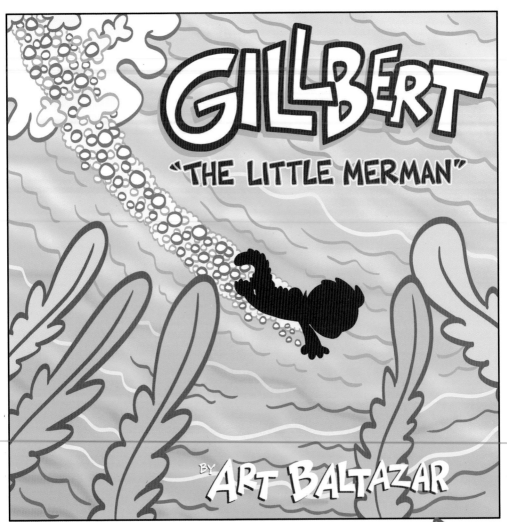

GILLBERT
"THE LITTLE MERMAN"

BY ART BALTAZAR

7

...AND SO FULL OF LIFE AND WONDER.

SNIFF

EXQUISITE.

WONDROUS PERFECTION.

SWIM SWIM

WHAT A BEAUTIFUL DAY IN **ATLANTICUS.**

WELL, THE SURFACE WORLD IS A MYSTERIOUS PLACE...

...FILLED WITH INTERESTING CREATURES...

...ON LAND...
...AIR...
...AND SEA.

SEA?

YES.

THESE CREATURES USE SHIPS AND BOATS TO FLOAT ON OUR SEAS.

THAT IS LIKELY WHERE YOUR MESSAGE CAME FROM.

11

MAYBE THEY ARE SENDING US A STORY?

MAYBE?

OR A POEM?

THE SURFACERS ARE FASCINATED BY THE FANTASTIC.

YET THEY FEAR THE UNKNOWN.

LIKE YOUR FRIEND NESSIE.

Y'KNOW, THEY'RE CALLING HER THE LOCH NESS MONSTER.

RIDICULOUS! THEY DON'T UNDERSTAND.

SHE GOES OUT FOR A LITTLE SWIM AND GETS CAUGHT ON CAMERA...

...THEN BECOMES A PLANETARY SUPERSTAR!

DO THEY KNOW ABOUT US?

LATER, IN GILLBERT'S ROOM...

HEY, GILL. WHAT'RE YOU DOING?

OH.

HI, SHERBERT.

I'M WAITING FOR **MOM.**

WE'RE GOING TO TRANSLATE THIS LETTER.

WHAT DO YOU HAVE SO FAR?

SO FAR...

...NOTHING.

14

15

26

MEANWHILE, IN DEEP SPACE...

...A FIERY ASTEROID IS ON A COLLISION COURSE WITH **EARTH!**

SPLASH

SSSSS

THUMP

32

A **SUB**-ATOMIC AWESOMATOR!

IT'S FROM THE **SURFACE**.

BUT MOST OF THE TIMES ...NOT!

IT GOES DEEP, BABY!

DEEP AND UNDER SLIP SLIDIN' COOL, DADDIO.

OKAY.

HEY, GILLBERT.

WANT TO SEE SOMETHING BEFORE YOU GO?

SURE.

LIKE WHAT?

FOLLOW ME.

IT'S JUST A BIT BEYOND THE SUB-ATOMIC AWESOMATOR.

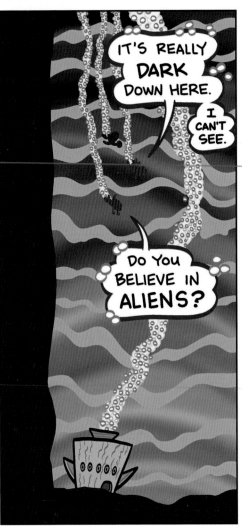

IT'S REALLY **DARK** DOWN HERE.

I CAN'T SEE.

DO YOU BELIEVE IN **ALIENS?**

HUH?

ALIENS?

YOU MEAN THE OUTER SPACE KIND?

YEP.

UM.

I THINK SO.

SOMETIMES.

PRINCE GILLBERT?

HI.

WHAT ARE YOU?

ME?!

OH. I'M CREEPLE!

YOU ARE GOING TO SEE LOTS OF THINGS YOU'VE NEVER SEEN BEFORE.

SHE'S RIGHT!

THE FOLKS DOWN HERE ARE UNKNOWN TO THE SURFACE WORLD.

LIKE US?

EXACTLY!

NOW... MAY WE SEE TEEQ?

OH, SURE.

GO RIGHT IN.

THANKS.

WOW.

THERE SURE IS LOTS OF CORAL.

THIS PLACE MUST HAVE BEEN HERE A LONG TIME.

HERE THEY COME!

HUH?

43

GREETINGS!

I AM TEEQ!

GOOD TO SEE YOU AGAIN, MISS PHIBIAN.

I SEE YOU FINALLY BROUGHT **HIM** TO VISIT ME.

YES.

GILLBERT, I'D LIKE YOU TO MEET **TEEQ**.

HELLO.

IT'S AN HONOR.

MY DAD SAYS THE **OCEAN** IS THE CENTER OF THE **UNIVERSE**.

NAUTICUS!

WELL, IF THAT'S THE CASE...

WELCOME TO THE **CENTER** OF THE **CENTER**.

C'MON... THERE IS SOMETHING YOU NEED TO SEE.

OKAY?

OKAY.

GILL, I REALLY THINK WE SHOULD BE GOING HOME NOW.

HEY!

WAIT FOR ME!

WHOA.

A LITTLE GROWTH SPURT, HUH?

WHAT'S GOING ON?

SHE SURE IS GROWING SUPER FAST.

I THINK WE MAY HAVE A DAUGHTER.

MORE GROWING?

53

CONCENTRATE.

FREE YOUR MIND.

HEAR MY WORDS.

ACCEPT MY THOUGHTS.

HE WILL BE THE FUTURE KING.

MEETING GILLBERT WAS WONDROUS.

THANK YOU, MISS PHIBIAN.

YOU'RE QUITE WELCOME.

HE WILL MAKE US PROUD.

HMM.

THIS MESSAGE...

GILLBERT?

HI, MOM.

YOU'RE HOME?

YEP.

OH, I SEE YOU STILL HAVE THAT SURFACE MESSAGE.

YEP.

HOW ABOUT WE DO SOME TRANSLATING?

OKAY.

MOM?

YES?

DO YOU KNOW TELEPATHY?

OOH!

WOW!

HOT!

THUNK

KSSSSS

WAIT A SECOND!

WHAT JUST HAPPENED?

PLOOP

"THEY HAVE BEEN STREAMING ACROSS THE UNIVERSE FOR CENTURIES..."

"...LOOKING FOR SOME PLACE **HOT** ENOUGH TO SUPPORT THEIR FIERY LIFESTYLE."

"PLUS, THE VOLCANO LEADS ALL THE WAY TO THE EARTH'S CORE."

"OH, THEY'LL BE PRETTY COMFORTABLE DOWN THERE."

C'MON. THERE'S A CELEBRATION GOING ON BACK HOME IN **ATLANTICUS**.

MOMENTS LATER...

LOOKS LIKE THOSE PYROCKIANS ENJOY MUSIC JUST LIKE WE DO!

KICK IT!

QUEEN NIADORA.

HELLO, TEEQ.

GOOD TO SEE YOU, OLD FRIEND.

WHAT A PARTY!

WHOA!

HERE WE GO AGAIN!

—MERMAN FOREVER!

WATCH OUT FOR PAPERCUTZ

Aw, yeah! Welcome to the grooviest graphic novel ever featuring an aquatic little green guy, GILLBERT #1 "The Little Merman," by Art Baltazar, from Papercutz, those fishy folks dedicated to publishing great graphic novels for all ages. I'm Jim Salicrup, the Editor-in-Chief and erstwhile stowaway on a yellow submarine, and I'm here to tell you a little bit about GILLBERT and Papercutz…

As already noted, GILLBERT is the creation of cartoonist Art Baltazar, a creator who has had great success creating comics for all ages. Let me interrupt myself to clarify exactly what I mean by this "all ages" stuff. Usually "all ages" is used as a euphemism for "just for kids." When we say it at Papercutz, we mean "all ages," as in we hope that someone as young as two (who will need someone to read the graphic novels to them) or as old as 102, and everyone in between, will enjoy our graphic novels. That's our goal. Do we always succeed? You tell us. Seriously, that's why we provide our contact info in that "Stay in touch!" box at the bottom of the page. Obviously some of our titles are enjoyed by more younger fans than others, but that's okay too. At Papercutz we publish a wide variety of graphic novels, some feature incredibly popular characters such as THE LOUD HOUSE, THE SMURFS, HOTEL TRANSYLVANIA, TROLLS, and many more, while others will feature characters you may have never met before, such as ERNEST & REBECCA, ARIOL, THE SISTERS, ANNE OF GREEN BAGELS, MANOSAURS, and many more. But they all respect your intelligence and are never written down to "kids." I've been lucky enough to not only hear from countless children who love Papercutz, but many adults as well. I believe that's because a good story is a good story, and a good story will appeal to everyone, which brings us back to Art Baltazar…

Copyright © 2017 Metaphrog.

I've been a big fan of Art's work for years, and I can't believe it's taken this long to get Art to create a new series for Papercutz. That may be because he's been writing and drawing so many other great comics (such as TINY TITANS, to name just one!), he's just been too busy. But we're nothing if not patient at Papercutz, and we think GILLBERT was worth the wait, and we hope you do too.

And speaking of waiting, while you wait for the second GILLBERT graphic novel—coming soon—may I suggest checking out another undersea graphic novel from Papercutz? It's a beautiful adaptation of HANS CHRISTIAN ANDERSEN'S THE LITTLE MERMAID by Metaphrog. Hey, if you enjoyed "The Little Merman," you'll like this non-Hollywood-style version of the classic tale. Oh, and there's another Papercutz graphic novel featuring a groovy little green guy, which even has a great cover by Art Baltazar, called GUMBY #1 "50 Shades of Clay." On the following pages, we're offering an exclusive excerpt—that just happens to take place partially undersea. We hope you like it, and check out the GUMBY graphic novel which features lots more stories with the lovable clayboy.

TM and © 2017 Prema Toy Co., Inc.

Gee, my fingertips are getting a little pruney, maybe it's time I return to the surface. But I do hope you return for GILLBERT's next great graphic novel, coming soon from… Papercutz!

Thanks,

STAY IN TOUCH!

EMAIL:	salicrup@papercutz.com
WEB:	papercutz.com
TWITTER:	@papercutzgn
INSTAGRAM:	@papercutzgn
FACEBOOK:	PAPERCUTZGRAPHICNOVELS
FAN MAIL:	Papercutz, 160 Broadway, Suite 700, East Wing, New York, NY 10038

By Veronica and Andy Fish

MY SON, **PRINCE OBELLO**, WAS TAKING THE ORB FOR ITS ANNUAL CLEANING, AS HE WAS WASHING IT IN THE OCEAN A **GUBBLE** WARRIOR ROSE UP AND SEIZED IT FROM HIM.

THE ORB DOES MORE THAN PROVIDE LIGHT AND COLOR..

IT INVIGORATES OUR ISLAND, IT SUSTAINS US AND PROVIDES US WITH OUR NORMALLY BOUNTIFUL FEASTS!

HE RETURNED SAFELY TO US, THANK GOODNESS, BUT THE ORB WAS **LOST** FOREVER.

NOW ALL WE HAVE ARE THESE FEW NUTS AND BEANS.

GOSH!

AND I COULD HAVE HAD A **CHICKEN POT PIE**...!

THE GUBBLES ARE A SINISTER AND EVIL LOT WHO HAVE WANTED WAR WITH US FOR GENERATIONS.

THEY ARE **VERY SCARY**-- WITH THE NO COLORS AND ALL.

HAVE YOU TRIED TALKING TO THEM?

THEY ARE **HORRID CREATURES** THAT CAN'T BE REASONED WITH!

WEREN'T YOU LISTENING? THEY HAVE **NO** COLORS!

HMMMM.

CHICKEN... POT... PIE...

GEE, KING, IF YOU'LL LET US USE TWO OF YOUR BOATS WE MAY BE ABLE TO HELP YOU OUT.

**Can't we all just get along? Find out in GUMBY #1
"50 Shades of Clay" available now wherever books are sold!**

MORE GREAT GRAPHIC NOVEL SERIES AVAILABLE FROM PAPERCUTZ™

THE SMURFS #21

THE GARFIELD SHOW #6

BARBIE #1

THE SISTERS #1

TROLLS #1

GERONIMO STILTON #17

THEA STILTON #6

SEA CREATURES #1

DINOSAUR EXPLORERS #1

SCARLETT

ANNE OF GREEN BAGELS #1

DRACULA MARRIES FRANKENSTEIN!

THE RED SHOES

THE LITTLE MERMAID

FUZZY BASEBALL

HOTEL TRANSYLVANIA #1

THE LOUD HOUSE #1

MANOSAURS #1

THE ONLY LIVING BOY #5

GUMBY #1